T0157505

Endorsements

The Oaf in Ophir rekindles the spirit of the forest for young and old to explore, trust, play and come back to time and time again. This children's story will prompt any age to grab a friend and go explore their surrounding ecosystem, one creek at a time.

—*Aimee Retzler, Sierra Harvest Co-Director*

With the magic that comes from being in tune with nature, this book sends all the messages I want my daughter to hear and take to heart. A thoroughly enjoyable read!

—*Corinne Lowell-Meigs, Teacher*

Creating wonder for youngsters is not as easy as it may seem. To feed young and fertile minds and hold their attention with a fresh story requires not only skill but also authenticity. Dan Linsteadt accomplishes this quite smoothly in his delightful book, *Oaf in Ophir*. Linsteadt's development of characters is remarkable—they come alive in just a few pages and they are bound to stay in the reader's imagination long after reading the book. The story is compelling and draws the reader along in a steady flow. It also contains an important message about our relationship with nature and its creatures. That message is folded neatly into the story without any preaching. Oh, to be a child discovering the magic of the woods and streams with the Oaf! I imagine anyone who reads this book will feel exactly that way.

—*John Bowman, Writer/Poet*

OAF
IN
OPHIR

DANIEL G LINSTEADT

BALBOA.
PRESS

A DIVISION OF HAY HOUSE

Interior Graphics/Art Credit: Stephen M Linsteadt
Book Cover Artwork credit: Lyda Linsteadt

Balboa Press books may be ordered through booksellers or by contacting:

Balboa Press
A Division of Hay House
1663 Liberty Drive
Bloomington, IN 47403
www.balboapress.com
1 (877) 407-4847

Print information available on the last page.

ISBN: 978-1-5043-6198-9 (sc)
ISBN: 978-1-5043-6199-6 (hc)
ISBN: 978-1-5043-6200-9 (e)

Library of Congress Control Number: 2016911215

Balboa Press rev. date: 02/08/2016

CONTENTS

I dedicate this book to my inquisitive grandchildren, beautiful children, loving wife, and supportive parents.

Chapter 1
Was That Him?

T he sky was powder blue above the hillside of granite outcrops, golden grass, and pine and oak trees whose contorted branches mingled under the high yellow sun. Emory's bare legs tingled in the cool water that flowed in braids through a smooth groove carved into a large white-and-black speckled slab. Mountain blue jays flitted from tree to grass with an occasional raucous shout when a neighboring jay got too close. He glanced to his right at a couple of kids, maybe going into fourth grade and about his age. He wanted to play with them as they screeched with delight while splashing in the shallow pool fed by a gurgling waterfall. Parents looked on with lazy eyes from the small strip of beach where coarse sand accumulated from the hillside. The steep ascent to the main trail above continued onward to a hidden waterfall. The falls, spilling for over thirty feet, had long been a stunning attraction for weekend hikers and tourists who learned of its location from the Ophir locals. A recently built wooden deck reached out over the rocks, where the waterfall's spray created a rainbow. The rushing water flowed into the larger stream just below where Emory rested. Feeling flushed from the sun and with hunger growling in his belly, he sat up, remembering when Grandma would relax next to him on this very rock. *I need to get home soon so she doesn't worry,* he reminded himself.

A flash of light and sudden movement up the hillside caught his eye. Trying not to blink, he saw a flutter behind a large oak he didn't remember being there before. "Is that you?" he asked, squinting.

The newspaper clippings his parents kept in a scrapbook back home, about an oaf living in Ophir, made him wonder. The many articles told of a magical oaf who was the cause of both concern and mystery for the locals. They described the good deeds that mysteriously occurred after sightings of this supposed homeless man, referred to as the Oaf. His picture had never been captured, but witnesses all said he appeared to be a bumbling man, who was also nimble while prowling their property near the streams.

Emory pulled his legs up into a crouch, ready to spring. Tilting his head to the side while staying focused on the oak tree, he listened for any sounds up the hillside. He heard only the babble of the stream and hikers chatting, but the jays remained quiet in the trees. *It's as if something is causing them concern,* he realized. He leaped across the spillway and landed softly on bare feet. Scampering up the warm rock, he peered over its ledge.

"Time to go home," a parent shouted above laughter.

"Thank you," Emory whispered, focusing on the ancient tree and wanting another glimpse. "Seeing the Oaf would make my three weeks with Baba magical."

What appeared to be an arm moved from behind the tree. He glanced back at his sports sandals sitting on the rock below and wished they were on his feet. Slipping over the weathered stone bright with patches of orange and pale-green lichen, he jumped from boulder to outcrop. He stopped with one knee touching the brown grass growing among broken branches, rocks, and the creeping myrtle that inched away from the shadows. He moved forward with tender feet and alert ears. The sounds of the stream and people became muted while the creak of branches and the rustle of leaves seemed heightened. Inch by inch, he climbed toward the tree.

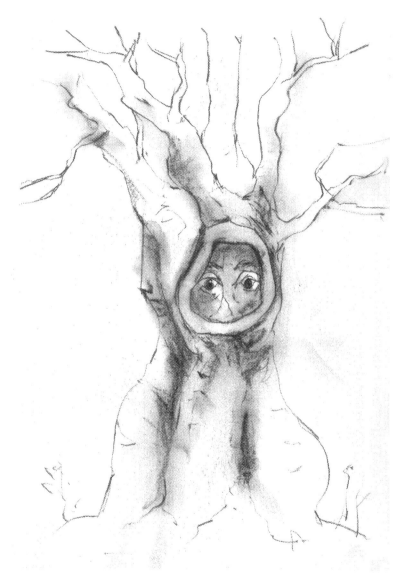

"Waaay," floated through the air in a deep, low voice. The sounds of the flick of fabric and the snap of wood twisting jolted Emory's heart. He sprang toward the tree and pressed his hand against the green moss that carpeted the gray bark. He peered behind the trunk and shouted, "Ouch!"

Breathing loudly, his heart pounding in his ears, he saw nothing. Rubbing his tender heel, bruised from a small rock, he glanced around with the word *way* resonating in his memory.

"Where did you go?" he asked.

Stepping behind the tree, imagining he was the Oaf, he watched the world down below. He wondered if the Oaf were afraid of what it had become. *How silent and different the view must have been over a hundred years ago,* he thought.

"He can't possibly move that fast," Emory whispered, peering around.

He studied the tree's creased, weathered bark. A large, gnarled knot swirled around where a branch once attached. "This will make an amazing painting," he said, wishing he had the camera. "Baba and I can paint it together."

He ran his fingers over the bark that weaved around like a wreath and decorated the exposed wood within. "I know you were here, but where did you go?" he asked, hoping the voice would answer. "No wonder your picture was never taken; you're magical, but someday I'll see your face."

Emory tiptoed down the hillside and soothed his soles in the cold water. Jumping to the small island, he slipped on his sandals and backpack while staring at the tree. "Way?" he repeated. "*Wwway.* Did I hear that right? It was a voice, not the wind; I'm sure of it."

He hopped over the stream and landed on the coarse sand with a crunch. Slipping through tree branches and blackberry creepers and clambering over large boulders, he began the long hike back to his bicycle.

"Baba will enjoy hearing about today's adventure," he said to himself. She liked the oaf stories but said it brought too many tourists to the town.

Chapter 2

Leave a Note?

Walking briskly in the middle of the narrow trail, as he eyed the dark-green, glossy leaves in groups of three, Emory remembered a valuable lesson: *poison oak is awful.* After he brushed against it a couple of years back, it had taken his skin a month to heal and longer for his legs to look normal again. Baba said she was the same, sensitive to its touch.

Emory never met his grandpa, but Baba said he could touch it without getting a rash. Baba and his parents didn't talk about him much; they always changed the subject.

The trail widened, but Emory was still wary of the poisonous bush that grew in bunches everywhere. The air was fresh with a hint of pine and the sweet scent of buckeye flowers. The soothing gurgle of the stream followed the trail only part of the way, while the moisture kept the air cool in the hot summer sun. As the trail and stream parted ways, the path became hot and dusty.

Emory loved visiting Baba's house. Three weeks was never enough. For Emory, having time in nature and away from friends was relaxing (and necessary) after the long school year. Back home, there were only rows of houses and apartments. There, the trees and bushes were crammed into tiny yards or neatly placed in the small neighborhood park.

The backpack slipped to the ground as he bent over to unlock his bike: twenty-four, seven, twenty-six, and click. Now the two-mile ride back to Baba's home through rural landscapes of rolling fields and irrigation ditches was before him. Houses were perched on the tops of small knolls or tucked into thick groves of trees. Horses, goats, and llamas grazed in many of the fenced properties. Emory had seen skunks, a fox, turkeys, geese, lots of deer, one donkey, a tortoise, and two great herons, but never the raccoons or possums that came out at night. Today he almost added the Oaf to his growing list.

The piece of cloth he briefly saw behind the oak tree had appeared worn. Somehow it made him feel sad for the Oaf. Living in the nooks and crannies of the open spaces that were slowly going away, like the deer, the poor creature had to eke out a living in rags.

Emory pedaled up the steep driveway of Baba's house, sad to have only a few days left before his parents would come to take him home. The smell of dinner wafted through the air as he leaned his bike against the old outdoor kitchen, now a storage shed. He never ventured in there because of the smell of rats and their long, hairless tails.

"Yuck!" he said with a shiver and walked up the stairs to the outdoor porch that sat up high, like a tree house.

Slipping off his dusty sandals, he looked out through the tree limbs. There was nothing better than sipping one of Baba's mandarin smoothies while watching the hummingbirds flit among the branches or catching a glimpse of one of the Koi rising to the surface of the small pond down below. Sometimes a hummingbird would suddenly hover, fluttering loudly in front of his face, with a look of intrigue. Satisfied he had nothing to offer, it would disappear as quickly as it appeared.

Emory stepped into the house and announced, "I have a great story to tell today, Baba."

"Good," she answered from the kitchen. "Go clean up. Dinner will be ready in ten minutes."

He took off his clothes and pushed them into a heap with his feet, like he was maneuvering a soccer ball. His bed was on the wall opposite Baba's desk, so he could look out the window facing the backyard. He peeked out, hoping to see a deer and her babies foraging, but they were not cooperating tonight. They usually sneaked through in the early morning.

Emory sat up straight and silent at the dinner table, his eyes closed. Baba loved to quietly pray, never asking for anything, but only giving thanks if she happened to speak. She looked up with her loving eyes, breaking the silence. "Dig in! I hope you like it."

"You know I love enchilada casserole—especially yours, Baba."

"So, tell me about your day," she asked.

"I started to read the book you gave me, but I nodded off after a few pages. It was a warm, lazy day, and the sound of the water is always so soothing."

"I understand," she said, taking a bite.

"I'll read some tonight. Anyway, the falls weren't that crowded today." His eyes widened. "You won't believe what happened!"

"Do tell," she responded with a grin.

"I was sitting with my feet in the water—you know, your favorite spot. I was staring at the hillside daydreaming, when I saw it."

"Saw it?" she asked, raising one eyebrow.

"Yeah, the Oaf!"

"Really?"

"Pretty sure."

"So, you didn't actually see him?"

"It had to be him. I snuck up the hillside to where he was hiding behind a tree. A piece of his clothing, from his arm, waved from behind the thick trunk, and he spoke."

"You heard him?" she asked, now with wide eyes.

"Yes!"

"What did he say?"

"Wayyy," he pronounced, slowly.

"Only one word?"

"Yeah, but the beginning wasn't clear, so it sounded more like 'way,' I think."

"Maybe he was telling you to go away," she said, with a wink.

"Maybe," he answered, playing with the word in his head to see if that could be right. "Anyway, I think he's a kind and gentle oaf. If he said that, it was because he wanted peace and quiet. You know how people can be so noisy and leave their trash behind. The newspaper stories tell of him being the one who cleans up after everyone during the night."

"That's true," Baba said, stroking her hair back and staring out the window. "So he's hanging out at the falls these days. That's a good place to be. There's a lot of empty space beyond the creek to roam and hide." She turned to Emory with laughing eyes. "Take some food for him tomorrow."

"You think he would eat it?" he asked, liking the idea. "How would I know he eats it and not some animal?"

"You won't, unless you see him."

"Can I sleep there tomorrow night and watch?"

"Not sure that's such a good idea, but fun to think about."

He took a large bite, filling his cheeks.

"Maybe you should leave a note with your name on it," she suggested, holding her full spoon in midair. "Maybe write your address on it."

"You think he can read? An oaf isn't very smart, after all."

She smiled. "Maybe he's smarter than you think—just pretending to be an oaf."

"Oh Baba, now you're kidding me."

She turned her gaze back outside at the large cedar, where a clothesline stretched from the house and often had clothes hanging to dry. "I can pack my favorite sandwich for you to give him." Mischief was in her eyes, not seen very often.

"You want to come with me?" he asked.

"No, I can't walk that far anymore, and it's too hot during the day. I'll leave this mission to you."

"You think he'd like your Swiss cheese sandwich laced with Hatch chili, tomatoes, and lettuce?"

She smiled. "I think he will love it. How can anyone not love that sandwich?"

"Well ..."

"Okay, not you, but that's because you don't know what's good for you yet. Someday you will love that sandwich." She pulled him in for a big hug. Pressing her hands over his chest, she added, "Your big heart tells me so."

Chapter 3

Lunch Bag

The next morning Emory slipped on his clothes from yesterday and walked into the kitchen. Baba was sipping her morning tea and pretended not to notice him. A white lunch bag and a note pad sat next to her.

"Good morning, dear one," she said.

"Good morning, Baba. Is this for the Oaf?"

"Yes. I didn't sleep well last night, so I thawed out the chili and made a sandwich." She glanced at Emory. "Made one for all of us."

He peered into the bag. "Thanks."

"You get to write the letter, but I had a thought. Instead of an address, why don't you put your name

16

and my name? You know, oafs aren't that smart, so an address wouldn't be of much use."

"You're funny, Baba!" He grabbed the notepad and began to write.

Dear Mr. Oaf,

Baba made you a sandwich. She thought you'd like it. If not, don't blame me. My name is Emory, and I want to meet you. I'm only here a few more days, so please don't wait too long.

Your friends, Emory and Baba

"You think he can read this?" he asked.

"You never know. Maybe, just maybe, he learned to read when he was young."

Emory laughed while placing the note carefully above the sandwich and folded the top of the bag twice. Setting the bag into the backpack, he added, "Wish me luck!"

"Good luck, and enjoy. Please be home a little earlier today. I worry when it gets too late in the day."

Emory pedaled briskly to the falls park, locked his bike, and skipped down the path feeling light and happy. The closer he got to the stream, the heavier his heart felt. The thought of actually meeting the Oaf scared him.

"Maybe he doesn't like kids," he said, gazing at the blue sky through green pine needles. "No, the Oaf always likes kids. He's just a kid in an adult body. That's what I think."

He climbed down the trail and quickly leaped onto the small island, glad it had not been occupied yet. A couple in quiet conversation walked by on the trail above to go see the hidden waterfall. He wondered when it would be the best time to place the bag by the oak tree. He decided toward the end of the day, so no one would see it and take it. He pulled his new book out of his backpack, settled back on the smooth rock, and began reading about wizards and magic.

After reading a couple chapters, he was too distracted by thoughts of the Oaf to enjoy the sorcery within the pages. Excited about the Oaf finding the lunch bag and reading the note kept his eyes lifting from the book. He conjured up images of how he looked—a hooked nose, round cheeks above a large bushy beard that hid the rest of his face except for fat lips, large, laughing green eyes, and bare feet that stepped silently without leaving a mark. They'd play hide-n-seek and sneak up on a family of deer without being noticed.

He placed the book down and waded into the water, then sat under the small waterfall so it massaged his shoulders. He allowed the current to carry him toward the small island, where he swam back to the falls to complete a full circle and did it all over again. Time passed blissfully as he warmed himself in the sun. Occasionally he moved to the shade so others could enjoy the island, but he was always aware of the hillside and the large oak tree. The sun crept across the empty blue sky. People came and went, leaving behind napkins, plastic bottles, and cigarette butts. He placed the trash in his backpack, hoping the Oaf was watching and approved.

Finally, the pool was empty of people, and Emory ascended the hillside. Stopping at the same oak tree he observed the day before, he surveyed the landscape for a good place to set the lunch bag. A boulder sticking out of the grass like a small iceberg floating in the ocean caught his eye. He placed the lunch bag on the stone, glee bubbling in his chest. After taking several steps away, he sat cross-legged and listened to the river, birds chirping, woodpeckers tapping on a branch, and the occasional conversation drifting by. He wondered what the Oaf liked to do during the day, where he slept, and how he stayed warm. He stared at the tree where the Oaf had hidden yesterday. To his surprise, the tree looked strangely different. After studying it carefully, he realized the knot was missing. Rising to his feet, curious if he was at the wrong tree, he hustled down the slope and looked back up, then down, and back up again. He knew it was the right tree; he was sure of it. Scampering back up to the ancient oak, he stood gawking at its gray bark where the knot had been. Confused, he rubbed his hand over the bark, feeling how hard and rough it was.

"Maybe I imagined everything yesterday. Too much sun played tricks on my mind."

"Thhhanks," a voice hushed through the trees.

Spinning around scared, Emory grabbed his backpack and stood perfectly still. "You're welcome," he responded, meekly.

He looked at the boulder; the lunch bag was gone. His heart skipped a beat, and his hands became clammy. Even the birds were still. Only the air shifted through the branches.

"I've got to go home now," he said in a quivering voice. "I'll see you tomorrow, okay? I hope you enjoy the sandwich." He backed up several steps, then turned and dashed down to the stream and jumped to the island. He turned, hopeful to see him, but no one was there.

"I should have stayed," he muttered. "Maybe he would have shown himself."

Chapter 4

Tree Knots

B ack at home, sitting at the dinner table, Emory announced, "I heard him again. He also took the lunch bag."

Baba stared at him. "You don't look very excited about this. Did he scare you?"

"Yes, I was scared," he said, nodding.

"Why, my darling?"

"He was right behind me, and I didn't even know it. He took the sandwich bag without a sound, and so quickly."

Baba regarded him with tender eyes.

"Something wasn't right," Emory continued. "The tree I saw him at yesterday changed. I'm afraid of him now."

"How did the tree change? You know there's always a good explanation for everything, right?"

"Yes, Baba, but this is magic."

Baba leaned back and folded her arms. "Magic? Okay, tell me how the tree changed."

"The beautiful knot was gone. I remember it vividly, because I wanted us to paint it."

"I see. Well, I think there's a good answer."

"You do?"

"Yes." She sat forward placing her elbows on the table. "The story I've heard is that the Oaf is magical. When he was a young man, he loved walking through the woods, especially old groves. One day he stumbled into a sacred Native American forest. All day he kept seeing movement out the corner of his eye, like someone was there watching him. It felt like a good presence, as if spirits were there protecting him. The next time he saw movement, he kept his eyes looking forward but observant of what was to his side. The presence didn't leave him, so he quickly glanced its way, but there still wasn't anyone there. He noticed that this always happened close to a large pine tree. Each tree had a knot as you described, like a wound from the past, but it had turned into something beautiful instead of an ugly scar."

"I've never heard of this before, or read it in any of Dad's clippings," Emory said, with wide eyes.

"No, I suppose you wouldn't have. This is only the growing folklore of the Oaf."

"But if it's true, then is the Oaf a spirit or the ghost of a tree?" He thought a moment. "So there can be many oafs, right? Lots of trees have knots. They would all have spirits."

"The knot of a tree is often a wound, but sometimes it can be a good spirit in hiding. They watch and protect the forest and help guide others that are also friends of the trees. I believe the Oaf is like those spirits."

"If the Oaf can turn into a beautiful knot, then is he a spirit?"

"I believe he is still alive and learned how to melt into a tree as a knot so he can watch the unaware."

"I did hear a strange noise the other day, like the twisting of bark or a branch. That must have been him turning into a knot, right? That explains how he disappears so fast."

"He was observing you, so you must be special." She wiped a moist eye.

"He took the lunch bag, and he'll read the note." Emory glanced out the window. "He could be outside right now, watching us." He shivered. "How do you know a regular knot from a magical one?"

"I'm not sure."

"The idea of being watched without knowing it … is creepy. I don't want to go into the forest anymore."

"Oh, sweetie, I'm sure he's watching the stream and protecting something there. Maybe he's protecting a family of deer, or a wounded animal, or the river from gold miners wanting to dig it up at night. Who knows, but he's not watching or following you to be creepy."

He pondered this for a moment. "You're right. What a great way to keep an eye on things." He stared at Baba. "So he's like the ancient spirits, but still alive. Protecting the forest and watching out for others."

"Yes. I'm sure of it."

"Okay, I like him again." A large grin grew on his face. "I think he'll like your sandwich. How often does he get a treat like that?" He frowned in thought. "What about the note?"

"What did you write?"

"That I want to meet him."

"Well, maybe that will wondrously be arranged."

Chapter 5

Beaver

Emory awakened feeling sad. A mama deer scampered through the far end of the backyard. Two spotted fawns followed behind her. Bent low at the window, he watched them nibble on violets that grew like weeds near the side yard fence. The neighbors' old horse stood chewing and watching. Emory glanced at the large pine tree, three old oaks, a maple, then the mimosa, and their trunks appeared normal. The deer slowly walked along the fence and disappeared behind the outdoor kitchen.

"I'm not sure I want to talk to the Oaf; see him yes, but not talk," he said, identifying his sadness. "The Oaf makes me nervous, sad, and happy all at the same time. I'll do something different today. Maybe that will help."

Baba was sweeping the porch when he stepped outside.

"Good morning," Baba said. "You slept in. I bet you were tired from yesterday."

"Yeah," he answered, stretching both arms and folding them behind his head. "I think I'll sit by the stream this morning and read more of your book."

"Sounds like a plan." She glanced at him with searching eyes. "No Oaf today?"

"Nawww," he drew out slowly.

"Be careful."

"I will." Walking down the steps, Emory stopped at the small pond. The water lilies floating on the surface were budding delicate purple flowers. The Koi were hidden in the dark water shaded by the trees.

Baba swept leaves, sticks, and moss fallen from the roof into the dust pan. She dumped the contents into a paper bag and stood holding the broom. "Be home for lunch?"

"You think the Oaf will be here today?" he asked. "Will he know how to find us from the note?"

"You never know," she said, beginning to sweep again. "It is a long walk for him, so maybe not."

Emory moseyed down the driveway with book in hand.

Baba watched him with a smile, and then glanced toward the overgrown lot, her face becoming stern. The stunted orchard of apple, pear, and plum trees struggling among the weeds and tangle of blackberry runners was a reminder of better times. Oaks, buckeyes, camellias, and cottonwoods needing their branches trimmed and removed stood like shabby soldiers in uneven rows. Hidden far back toward the feeder stream was a small wooden shed. Naked fence posts and pieces of chicken wire lay held down by the tall grasses. Her eyes narrowed at the worn path the deer used as they came up from the stream to forage. She released a shallow breath, then turned to see Emory disappear down the slope, where the small waterfall tumbled and echoed all the way up to the porch.

Emory scampered down the slope and past an old couch that had become springs and a metal frame. Studying each tree trunk, he felt a little spooked. Holding his breath at the sight of a beaver standing on a narrow ledge below the waterfall, he watched it tugging at leaves from a small tree growing on the bank. The beaver sat with its large, flat, glossy tail between its legs and chewed with two bucked teeth. It waddled up a large rock that sheltered the small ledge and then dove into the turbulent water. Immediately, it popped out of the churning water and came down with a splash and floated away in the strong current.

"Now that is magical," he said out loud. "I get to add a beaver to my animal list."

Joy bubbled inside him as he stepped over the masonry channel used to divert water to a neighbor's home and walked along the smooth stones with perfect balance. Leaping onto the boulders that formed the natural dam creating the wide waterfall, he listened to its continuous roar as it drowned out the world in a soothing and hypnotic way. Slipping off his sandals, he dipped his bare feet into the calm, swirling water that hesitated before spilling over the ledge. Seeing where the feeder stream entered ahead, there was an enormous fig tree with new leaves bursting forth. He wanted to climb that tree someday. Opening the paperback book, he began to read.

The Oaf slipped stealthily toward the stream. He bent slowly to his knees, ready to spring, and gaped at the little boy. A tear pooled, and he buried his head into his rags. Quickly looking up, he scanned the surroundings. Rising to full height, he melted into the thick oak tree with perfect sight of the waterfall.

Chapter 6

Close Call

Sleep washed over Emory's warm body. He dog-eared the current page in the book and stood, stretching. Thirst and hunger gurgled in his belly, so he slipped on his sandals and maneuvered back to the stream's edge. He began the trek back up the slope when he heard, "Hello."

Jerking to his left, he saw the Oaf standing in front of a row of oak trees along the bank. His tattered clothes and long, matted hair were the same gray as the bark, but his face was clean and bright. He was tall with broad shoulders, and his smile was infectious behind a wooly beard.

"I enjoyed your note," he said in a clear, deep voice.

"How did you find me here?" Emory asked nervously, but not frightened.

"I know Baba. She has lived here a long time," he answered.

"That sneaky Baba," he whispered to himself.

"That she is," he said with a laugh.

Emory wanted to touch him, get close enough to smell his scent, so he took a step forward.

The Oaf took a side-step, and a sunbeam crossed his shoulder.

"You seem intelligent, not an oaf at all. Are you homeless?" Emory continued questioning him. "How did you learn your magic?"

The Oaf's forehead raised, eyeballs widened, and he tilted his head back.

"I'm scaring you, aren't I? I'm asking too many questions."

With a large bound, the Oaf plunged into the swift current and disappeared downstream, just like the beaver.

Emory stared in disbelief. "How could I be so dumb, asking so many questions like that? I should have reached for his hand or let him do the talking." He plopped down, tingling with excitement, but also sad. "Will he ever let me see him again?" He sat up straight. "He said he liked my note, so he can read. He's pretending to be an oaf, or more likely, people call him that because he lives in nature and not in a house." Springing to his feet, he dashed to Baba's home.

Emory quickly devoured a peanut butter and honey sandwich and washed it down with grape juice. Baba was taking a nap, so he quietly closed the door behind him. Slipping back on his shoes, he skipped down the driveway, buzzing with excitement. Gazing at the stream, he hoped to see the Oaf waving. Glancing to his left at the overgrown lot, he decided to explore there. Maybe the Oaf lived there at one time; someone must have. He sauntered down the deer trail and stopped at the small stream where the large fig tree on the opposite bank was in view. He made his way in the opposite direction toward the small, dilapidated house, which was only the size of a single bedroom. Blackberry vines stabbed at his bare legs, and barbed seeds stuck into his socks, causing his ankles to itch with each step. Finally reaching the wooden structure, he looked around, disappointed. Nothing indicated anyone ever lived here, unless it was a very long time ago.

Suddenly a tingle traveled down his spine, causing him to freeze and listen intently. "The Oaf has come back to talk to me," he whispered. He sensed a presence close by, watching. "Should I turn to greet him or wait for him to say hi?" His heart thumped wildly as he held perfectly still, feeling like a match flame and trying to not flicker. "Why doesn't he say something?" Unable to take the suspense any longer, he slowly turned, hoping not to frighten him.

A sudden flash of yellow eyes, large paws, and teeth sprang toward him. He screamed just as another body slammed into the outstretched mountain lion inches from his face. Emory wilted to the ground as two bodies crashed into the brush and then tumbled into the stream with a splash.

"Emory!" Baba shouted from her porch.

Emory's body twitched with fear. Unable to move or cry out, tears trickled down his cheeks. A hawk screeched in the branches high in a towering pine tree. The rustling of grass got louder, and closer.

"Emory, where are you?" Baba shouted.

"Here," he answered, faintly.

"There you are," Baba said, bending down to lift him. "What happened? Are you all right?"

He began to sob.

"What frightened you so, my dear?"

Taking a deep breath, he answered, "A mountain lion attacked me."

Baba stared with mouth open. She took hold of him and scanned the surroundings. "I think not. A mountain lion would not miss if it attacked. You must be mistaken. There haven't been lions this way in years."

"I saw its yellow cat eyes and large claws. Something sprang from nowhere and grabbed it. I heard them fall into the creek with a splash."

Baba squeezed Emory's shoulders. "The Oaf saved your life." She peered toward the stream. "I'm sure of it." She looked into his eyes. "Now you know why he has been watching you. The Oaf knew. He knew danger was stalking you."

"But he only came here because of the note. He said he knew your name."

"He spoke to you today?" she asked, with large eyes.

"Yes, but I frightened him away."

"Well, thank goodness he came back."

"Is he okay?" Emory asked. "I hope he isn't hurt. Can you see them in the stream?"

"I'm sure he's fine." She took his hand and led him back to the house. Stopping at the porch steps, she said, "You're special to him, you know." She looked away.

"You're crying?"

"Yes my love, I am. He knows who you are."

"What?"

"Go and clean up for dinner." She nudged him into the house.

Through the screen door, Emory heard her say, "Thank you, my love."

Chapter 7

Good-Bye

It had been two days since the lion attacked. Emory remained close to the house, mostly sitting on the porch reading and watching the birds and deer. He sat at the dinner table remembering the lion's yellow eyes and the Oaf coming to his rescue. He looked at Baba eating quietly and wondered why she said the Oaf was her love.

"I can see you have questions churning inside your busy head," Baba said. "When are you going to ask me your questions?"

He took the last bite of broccoli from his plate. "How will we know if the Oaf is okay? If he's hurt, or worse, I'll never forgive myself."

"My gut tells me he is doing fine, even the mountain lion," Baba answered. "Most likely, they immediately went in separate directions. He'd never hurt the lion."

"But how can I truly know?"

"Someday you will see him again, maybe next year. You'll come and visit me again, right?"

"Yes, of course, but waiting an entire year will haunt me. I can't get the cat's eyes out of my head, and the wondering, that's the hardest." They sat in silence, each in their own thoughts. Emory finally got the courage to ask, "I heard you the other day."

"Heard what?" Baba asked.

"You said the Oaf was your love."

"Oh, you heard that, did you?"

"Yes, sorry. I didn't mean to eavesdrop."

"Well, where do I begin?" She took hold of his hand and looked tenderly into his eyes. "The Oaf is your grandfather, your Bapa."

Emory gaped at her in disbelief. "How can that be?"

"Well, he's my husband, and still is."

"He left you?"

"No, more of a mutual agreement, but not because we didn't love each other; we still do. He wanted, more like needed, to live differently—to be away from the craziness of the world and its rules, and lack of love for animals, the trees, and land. He worked hard to buy this home and raise our kids. He was successful playing the game, but his heart ached, his soul yearned, and one day he just couldn't participate anymore. Some say he had a breakdown; I say he had enlightenment." She laughed, hiding tears she wiped from her eyes.

Emory's head spun, but he now understood why the Oaf would know where Baba lived. He now loved the Oaf more than ever and wanted to run into his arms. "I must see him before going back home. I want to live like him ... maybe." With moist eyes, he looked up at Baba. "He's my Bapa."

"I'll call you if I see him again," Baba said, hoping to reassure him. She watched Emory hold back tears. "Sometimes he appears on the deer path, where I see him kneeling down low and looking up at the porch."

"Really?" he asked.

"Someday, maybe he will join me on the porch again." Baba laughed with a tear trickling down her cheek.

"He must miss your mandarin smoothies," Emory said, feeling sad for Baba.

Baba only nodded.

"What if we all lived like the Oaf?" he asked. "I think the world would be much different—a more beautiful, kind, and friendly place."

"Yes it would," Baba said, squeezing his hand. "Yes, it would."

Before going to bed, Emory wrote his Bapa a letter:

Dear Bapa,

I'm proud to be your grandson. I'll keep your secret so no harm will come. Next year, please spend time with me. I want to hear everything you're willing to share. We can meet by the stream, where the beaver stops to

> *rest. Baba can come too, and we can have a*
> *picnic with her favorite sandwich.*
>
> *I love you, Emory*

Emory awoke feeling happy. He crept to the window and watched the deer eat while they felt safe. Baba was sitting outside on the porch eating a bowl of oatmeal when Emory finally left his room. He filled his bowl and joined her. The birds were singing, and even a frog joined in.

"Well, another visit comes to an end," Baba said, softly. "Your parents will be here soon."

"Maybe next year I can stay longer," he responded.

"I'd like that."

He handed Baba the note. "Please give this to Bapa, when you see him next."

She smiled but did not take the note. "I think someone is waiting to say good-bye down by the stream."

"Really!" he said, jumping from the chair and almost hitting his head on the low ceiling. He gaped at Baba.

"Go!" she said, like the start of a race.

Emory dashed down the driveway and almost tumbled down the slope. Slowing to a walk, not wanting to scare him away, he stopped at the edge of the stream and waited. The air smelled sweet with blackberry flowers beginning to blossom. A soft tap touched his shoulder. He turned and buried his face into the Oaf's arms. He smelled of pine and sage. His chest rose and fell, and Emory felt safe and happy in his embrace. Emory looked up into his moist eyes that peered down through shaggy hair and full beard.

"I love you Bapa."

"I love you too," he said, softly. A car honked loudly, and he stepped back.

"Sorry, that would be my parents." Emory thought a moment. "You want to see them, don't you?"

He smiled and patted Emory's head.

Emory held out the note. "This is for you."

The Oaf gently grasped it with two large, strong fingers and pressed it to his chest. They looked into each other's eyes, and Emory reluctantly turned to leave.

Turning back to say good-bye one last time, the Oaf was gone. Emory scanned the trees and saw a beautiful knot swirling in the large oak tree that stood tall by the stream, and smiled.

Chapter 8

Faye

Emory galloped up the driveway lined with deer-resistant chrysanthemums, hyssop, lavender, and sages, all shaded by tall oaks, pines, and cedars. Between just having hugged the Oaf and his parents arriving, his heart pounded excitedly.

As he approached the back of the station wagon, a cheer rang out. "Emory!"

Hidden behind a tall, blooming blue sage, Faye jumped out grinning, with leaves and grass already stuck in her hair. He cringed as she bounded toward him with arms spread wide. Wrapping her arms around him, she smelled of sage and fresh cut grass. She kissed his cheek and quickly skipped back to the flowers.

Laughter from the house mingled with the chirping of robins, cooing of doves, and the tap-tap-tapping of a woodpecker. He shuffled over to Faye; she was softly humming "row, row, row your boat" and sniffing newly picked flowers.

"Did you miss me?" Emory asked.

"Merrily ... yes ... merrily," she sang.

"I have a secret," he whispered in her ear.

Frowning, she became silent. "I don't like secrets."

"You'll like this one."

"Then tell me," she said, placing hands on her hips.

"I saw the Oaf!"

She stared at him with her mouth ajar.

"Ha, ha, that's a first," he said, laughing. "Faye has nothing to say."

"The Oaf is real?" she asked, nervously looking down the driveway.

"Yep, and there's more."

"I don't want to hear more. You're just trying to scare me." She dashed toward the house and up the stairs.

"Good, you're here," Baba said, poking her head out the door just as Faye streamed in. "Come in and have lunch. Your parents have good news."

Full from sandwiches, olives, carrots, celery, and watermelon, Baba stood to make an announcement.

"Emory, Faye, your parents will be leaving both of you with me for another week."

Emory's ears turned pink with exhilaration.

"But I don't want to stay here!" Faye shouted. "I'm scared of the O—"

"Ophir!" Emory interrupted. He glared at Faye, and she frowned back.

"There's nothing to be afraid of here at Grandma's," Baba said, hugging her. "We can have a picnic at the stream and make your favorite peach pie for dessert. I can take you and your brother swimming at the recreation center, if you like. You loved that last time, remember?"

Faye nodded and snuggled her stuffed black-and-white kitten into her neck. She glanced at Emory with a scowl.

Clutching her stuffed kitten, Faye watched from the door as her parents got into the car. Emory snuck up behind and tapped her shoulder. "You sure you don't want to see the Oaf?"

"No," she said, dipping her shoulder so his hand slipped away. "I want to be with Baba and swim." She glared at him. "I want to eat pie and look for deer and skunks and foxes."

"I bet this will change your mind. The Oaf is your—"

She dashed out the screen door and down the steps before he could finish his sentence.

Chapter 9

Moving Knot

Emory sprinted down the stairs and stood at Faye's side. He waved good-bye as his parents drove away. His mom's arm reached out the window and waved back. The sound of the engine slowly succumbed to the churning stream hidden down below.

"How about we play at the ravine?" Baba suggested. She picked up a folding chair and bottle of water already prepared and waiting.

Faye released Baba's leg and followed her, swinging her stuffed kitten.

Emory skipped ahead. He hustled down the trail and stopped to gaze at the oak tree. The large swirling knot was now gone. He glanced at all the trees, let out a long huff, then headed for the stream. Finding a flat, oval stone, he tossed it into the current and it was swallowed up.

Baba unfolded the chair and settled into it. She took off her sandals, rolled up her pants, and leaned back with a long sigh. The cool breeze wicking off the water soothed her hot skin exposed to the patches of sunlight. Peering at the large oak tree that reached out over the stream, she puckered her lips and made a smooch sound. The center of a large knot slowly opened and closed. She glanced at Faye before her heavy eyelids came together.

Faye hummed at the base of the oak tree, where orange calendula and purple creeping myrtle flowers glowed in the shadows. She picked one of each and placed them in the kitten's lap. Picking up small sticks, she bent them so they slightly broke. Leaning them together so they made up a small house, she picked two more flowers and placed them inside. The knot slid around the tree trunk so it was directly above her. She stopped construction and frowned. Looking up at the tree, she reached out and caressed the rough bark. She looked over at Emory tossing a large rock into the water with a kerplunk. Breaking off a section of creeping myrtle, she began humming again. The knot slid down a little more. Faye giggled.

Baba peeked over at Faye and grinned.

The knot slid down a few more inches. Faye stopped humming and held perfectly still. A large grin grew on her face.

"Hi, mister tree," she whispered. "I'm using your baby branches to build a fairy house. Do you like it?" She glanced at the knot just above her head and rose to her knees. Poking her finger into the middle of the knot, she said, "Does this tickle?"

The knot squeezed her finger, and she quickly retracted her hand. Jumping to her feet and taking a step back, she frowned at the knot.

"Are you okay?" Baba asked, standing.

"The tree bit me," she answered.

"Did it hurt?"

"It felt funny." She turned to poke it again, but the knot was gone. Scrunching up her nose and scratching her head, she patted the tree. "Please play with me some more." She placed her ear to the tree and listened.

"What are you doing?" Emory asked, standing next to her.

"I'm listening to the tree."

He studied the creases in the bark. "Did it talk?"

"No, but it was watching me."

"What does that look like?" he asked.

"Like a tree eye, but now it's closed."

"Let's head back home," Baba said, walking past them. "I've had enough sun for one day."

"But!" they both whined.

"I promise you can spend all day here tomorrow. Right now, I need your help. We need to prepare your beds."

"And kitten?" Faye asked.

"Yes, kitten's bed too."

She skipped over to Baba and took her hand. Emory walked around the tree, hoping to see a knot. Pursing his lips, he caught up with Baba and Faye.

Chapter 10

Leaf Boats

After eating breakfast, Emory and Faye skipped down the driveway.

Baba called out, "Emory, keep an eye on your sister."

"I will," he shouted back. He gave Faye a slight bump. "Now do what I tell you. Baba says so."

Faye ran ahead and scampered down the hill toward the stream. She headed straight for the oak tree. Standing next to her small house built yesterday was a larger house also made of sticks and creeping myrtle. Sitting with legs splayed out, she inspected the new home.

Emory knelt down next to her. "Wow!" The sticks were bent at ninety degrees, but not broken. Creeping myrtle vines wound around each section like a wicker basket. He grabbed the top and lifted it.

"Put it down!" Faye yelled. "It's mine!"

He sat it back down, noticing it didn't fall apart or even bend at the joints. "The Oaf must have made this."

"Really?" she asked, cautiously touching it.

"Yep, who else could've made a house like this?"

"A fairy," she responded. "It's a fairy house."

"Yeah! Made by the Oaf." He glanced around. "He's around here, somewhere."

Faye jumped to her feet and grabbed hold of his arm.

"There's nothing to be afraid of; he's family."

"Like Baba?"

"Like Bapa," Emory added.

"Bapa?" Letting go of his arm, she sat next to the stick house and hummed. She picked a purple flower and placed it inside.

"You okay?" he asked.

She ignored him while adorning the fairy home with flowers.

"Guess so," he muttered, turning toward the stream.

Stepping over the masonry channel, he advanced along the fitted stones and came to a stop next to the falls. Glancing at Faye, he smiled, then swung his legs around to face the oncoming current. The fig tree's leaves were now fully open. Memories of hugging the Oaf danced in his head as the hypnotic lapping and churning of the river kept his dreaming alive.

A sudden feeling of agitation surged through him as he glanced over his shoulder. Faye was gone! He jumped up and sprinted over the rocks, then leaped onto the bank. Reaching the top of the hill, he frantically looked around. Bounding to the driveway, he stopped and peered down the deer trail.

"Maybe," he whispered. He dashed down the trail and stopped at the creek, where Faye was talking to herself next to the bank. Relieved, he rushed to her. "Faye! Why did you leave without telling me?"

"I tried," she said, poking a hole in the center of a leaf.

That was dumb, he thought to himself. *Of course I couldn't hear her. She wouldn't have been able to reach me either.* He watched as she bent the stem and poked it through the hole. She placed a dandelion flower on the small leaf boat and sat it in the water. It bobbed up and down in the current and disappeared. "Where did you learn that?"

"In school." She picked up another leaf.

Still looking downstream, he spotted the fig tree. "I'm going to climb that tree. You stay here. You hear me?"

"Yes," she said, folding the leaf.

"Promise?"

She looked up at him. "Yes."

"Okay." He stepped into the cool, knee-deep water and waded across. Stepping on the far bank, he called back, "Stay right there. I'll only be a few minutes."

She placed another boat in the stream and watched it float away.

He skipped over rocks and slipped between bushes until he reached the spreading tree. Low branches bent back and forth while several leaves wiggled in the current. He maneuvered through the dense leaves and grabbed hold of the thick trunk. Grasping the first branch within reach, he hauled himself up and took hold of another thick limb. Poking his head out into the sunlight, he looked down at the merging tributaries. The smaller creek, its bubbling ripples rising and falling with flashes of light, gracefully bent toward the waterfall. He glanced back at Faye, who was rocking back and forth with knees almost touching her ears as she constructed a new boat.

Faye spotted a golden object sparkling in the stream bed where long grasses waved side-to-side. She reached forward and dipped her arm into the embracing water. Leaning forward a little more, she made a big grab. The ledge crumbled under her feet, and she tumbled in. Taking a quick breath, a little water still in her nose, she went under again, feeling her nostrils burn. A rock thumped into her back just as a large hand wrapped around her belly and lifted her up. Sputtering and blinking, she felt two hands holding her in the air. She opened her eyes and saw two large hazel eyes gazing back. Before she yelped, a hand covered her mouth.

"Please don't shout," a deep and pleasant voice said out of a mouth surrounded by a shaggy beard. "We don't need Baba to come running down here afraid and upset." He pulled back his large hand, saying,

"You'll also scare the mama and baby deer just across the creek."

Faye rubbed her nose and choked back tears.

The Oaf sat her gently down and moved her long, dark hair out of her eyes. "Do you want to see the deer?"

She nodded with trembling lips.

He tucked her under his arm and stepped into the water. "Be very quiet." Bending at the knees, he walked stealthily along the bank. He stopped before a thick grove of new-growth elms and pointed. "In there," he whispered. "They're snuggling."

Peering through the branches and seeing nothing, she shook her head.

The Oaf held out his hand with fingers pressed together, then slowly spread them apart. The limbs ahead slowly moved outward without a sound. Peering through the new window, she saw the mother deer licking her spotted fawn. Looking back at the Oaf with wide eyes, she smiled. Large white teeth grinned back.

Emory looked toward Faye and saw she was no longer by the stream. "She promised!" he shouted. "If she goes

back home without me, Baba will be upset." He scurried
down the tree and stopped in his tracks. He saw the Oaf
standing in the stream and holding Faye.

The Oaf retraced his steps and placed her down
at the stream's edge. He took a large cottonwood leaf
and folded one end. He tore the sides of the fold and
tucked the two new pieces together so they bent the
leaf upward. He did the same on the other end, which
caused the sides to curve upward. Placing an acorn in

the center, he handed the boat to her. She sat it in the water, and it sailed away.

Emory stopped, his heart beating at the sight of the Oaf.

The Oaf looked up and winked.

Emory bounded across the creek and wrapped his arms around him.

Faye grabbed hold of his leg and squeezed.

Squatting down, the Oaf asked, "Want to play upstream?"

"Yes!" they both shouted.

The Oaf covered his ears. "Too loud. You must be as quiet as a fox." He smiled. "Even more quiet. Can you do that?"

They both nodded.

"Great." He lifted them up onto his back with hands clasped behind him. They both sat comfortably on his arms as they observed over his shoulder while holding onto his mane. Stepping into the stream, he leaped to the bank, then, without a sound, back onto a rock poking out above the water.

Chapter 11

Garbage Can

The Oaf stopped and quickly lifted his chin twice. Looking in the direction he was facing, the two children saw a heron standing perfectly still in the stream. Its long legs were slightly bent and its large, sharp beak ready to strike. The blue-gray body blended into the background of oaks and blackberry bushes as it waited for a meal to swim by. After observing the bird for several minutes, Emory and Faye began to wiggle on the Oaf's back. The heron turned its head slightly before spreading its wings and rising into the air. With only the soft sound of air beneath large wings, it majestically flew above the stream and disappeared.

"Sorry," Emory whispered.

"Remaining still is not an easy task," the Oaf said. "It's a necessary skill, one not taught to children. Would you like to learn?"

Faye nodded while yanking on his long hair.

"Not unanimous, so lessons another time. Want to keep going?"

"Yes," they both answered.

Moving more slowly, the Oaf stepped quietly through the stream and past homes built almost on top of it. Faye rested her head on his shoulder and sniffed his musty scent, which reminded her of sweat and fresh clover when crushed between her palms. Her eyes grew heavy in the warm air as she moved with his body and listened to the gurgles of the stream. The Oaf suddenly stopped, and his broad shoulders drooped. He bent at the knees and released the children onto a narrow, sandy bank. Remaining on his haunches, he shook his head with a sigh. They all gaped at the bottles, cans, and chip bags littering the stream along the bank and further back into the trees.

"This is ugly," Emory said, breaking the silence. "Should we clean it up?"

The Oaf lifted a beverage can that had been submerged and poured out the water. "Yes, we must."

He emptied out another can as Emory and Faye began picking up the trash along the bank and placing it in a pile where the trail leading to the stream widened. Another wet can was tossed onto the growing mound as more wrappers and bags were found further back on the trail that eventually led to a seldom-used road. The Oaf followed the trail and inspected fresh tire tracks and footprints that had crushed the delicate grasses and flowers that bordered the edges. Glancing around, satisfied with the cleaner place, he sat next to the heap of rubbish. "It saddens me to see the beautiful elements of our planet being transformed by our unsavory alchemy, which further depletes its resources and energy reserves."

"What?" Emory asked.

"I'm talking to myself," the Oaf answered. He jumped up and looked in the direction of a house. He lifted the children and carried them to the other side of the stream and sat them down among a cluster of Spanish broom bushes bursting with yellow flowers. "Stay hidden. You can observe everything from here. I'll be back with a plan on how to get the trash removed." He winked. "Should be fun!" He patted each soft head, then crossed the stream.

Faye settled back and held out her hand, pinching her fingers together. She stared hard at two limbs and opened her fingers. She tried again while frowning and puckering her lips, hoping that would help.

"What are you doing?" Emory asked.

"Trying to move the branches."

Emory shook his head.

The Oaf followed a worn path leading toward the large, white house. The trail opened up into a wide field of grass where an old tractor was slowly rusting and a few tires lay scattered about. Walking next to a man-made pond full of cattails, across a manicured lawn, and past the front door, he stopped at the side of the house, where a black trash can with wheels sat waiting to be used. He peered inside and was glad it was empty. He lifted it and carried it past the front door before setting it down on the lawn. Grabbing the handle, he began to wheel it across the lawn so the lid and wheels rumbled with a racket. He looked toward the sky and sang with a booming voice.

"O da do da dee, I'm just a simple dummy."

"What are you doing?" a man shouted from a side window.

The Oaf ignored him while singing and pulling the trash can in a staggered line.

"Bring my trash can back, you stupid oaf!" the man yelled. "I'll have the police here to finally take you away!"

The Oaf slowed down and sang louder, "O da do dee, trash I do see, on your land, o da do dee."

The man dashed across the lawn in pursuit. The Oaf sped up, still wobbling in a curved line and singing at the top of his lungs.

Emory and Faye listened to the Oaf singing and gawked at each other. The Oaf came into view, and they giggled at his display of silliness with his arm swinging, head tilted back in song, and walking in a zigzag line. As the man chasing him got closer, the Oaf quickly shifted to the side and skipped ahead with the trash can bouncing and the lid clattering. The man readjusted and came after him again. The Oaf suddenly stopped and the man bounced off the trash can and fell to the ground, mumbling. Scurrying ahead until reaching the trail to the stream, the Oaf flopped down next to a pile of live oak leaves while releasing the trash can so it tumbled down the path and landed next to the mound of trash.

The man stopped out of breath and kicked leaves onto the Oaf. "You stupid old oaf, get off my property! You're nothing but a nuisance!" He lifted the trash can upright and yelled, "Look at this mess! If I found out you've been living here and making this mess ..." He stopped midsentence, seeing the Oaf was gone.

Sliding up next to Emory and Faye, the Oaf watched with a beaming grin.

"That was brilliant," Emory whispered. "That man was mean to you. I don't like that."

"It's all part of the game." He patted Emory on the head. "It's okay."

Faye took hold of his arm as they watched the man pick up all the garbage, then wheel the trash can back to his house, muttering the whole way.

Chapter 12

Bees

Emory popped up in bed with the morning light glowing pink outside the window. "I wonder what we'll do today."

"I want to pet a deer," Faye said with a yawn. "I want to move flowers from a distance, like the Oaf."

"You saw him do that?" he asked, pulling on his shirt. "He is magical."

Baba sat at the table sipping tea. "Good morning, you two scruffy ones. How did you sleep?"

"Good," Emory answered, sitting at the table. "I always sleep great here."

"Maybe because you run around all day in the sunshine," Baba said.

Faye took a bite of toast with a frown.

"How are you, my dear?" Baba asked her.

"Thinking."

"About?"

"Where the Oaf sleeps."

"Have you been playing with the Oaf?" Baba asked.

"Yes," she said, grinning. "I like him."

"So do I," Baba said. She pinched Faye's cheek, and they laughed.

Emory and Faye scampered down the deer trail and sat next to the creek. "I wonder how long we have to wait," Emory asked.

Faye held her arm out and pinched her fingers together. The sun slowly rose and warmed the air. Birds chirped hidden in the branches. A squirrel scurried up a tree, ran along a limb, and jumped to another tree branch. She stared at the water sparkling in the current as it undulated and bubbled along.

He tossed a rock into the stream.

"Stop that!" she protested.

"He's not coming today," he said, sitting down.

She sat up tucking her legs together with a frown. "Don't move."

"What?"

"The Oaf likes to watch. Maybe he's watching us."

"Ahhh," he said. "He'll like us practicing." He sat up, too. "Good idea for a little sister." Staring at the current, he saw an occasional leaf and stick float by. An itch burned into his neck, so he slowly reached up and scratched.

"That's a start," the Oaf said, behind them.

They both jumped up and gave him a big hug.

"So, how is *moving flowers* coming along?" he asked.

"Teach me!" Faye yelped.

"Okay," he said, bending down to her level. "Frowning won't help. You need to relax and imagine your fingers can extend to your desire. See how a slight puff of wind will bend the stalk and ruffle the leaves. Be like the breeze, and float through the air toward the flower.

Caress the delicate petals with your fingertips. It will move once you feel it."

"I can't do it," she said.

"Be patient and practice. Like riding a bike, it's hard at first. Once you get the hang of it, it's easy."

She held her hand up close to her eye and moved her fingers. "I feel it!" she announced after one minute. "Why doesn't it move?"

"Well I can't," Emory blurted out.

The Oaf cupped his hand on her head. "You both have gifts. Keep practicing and it will happen." He stood. "Now, I want to show you my friends today."

"A deer?" she asked.

"Deer are my friends, but today we'll visit very small and important creatures that need our help." He bent down, and they both hopped onto his back. "Ready?"

"Ready!" they both yelped.

He sped down the stream like an antelope bounding across a prairie. Slowing down, he stopped for a moment and admired the clean stream bed and surroundings that were full of trash yesterday. Continuing, they sped under a bridge and the foliage thickened. The Oaf walked slower while twisting and bending to avoid smacking into a branch or hitting a twig. Sweat beaded on his neck as they skirted past a few large homes. The stream widened, but the canopy above was full of leaves and branches so only small patches of light flickered on the ground. Finally stopping, he bent down, and Faye and Emory slid off his back. "This is one of my sanctuaries."

Emory studied the large boulders on the far side of the large pool, noting they would be great for jumping into the water. Water cascaded down rounded rocks into the pool, then spilled out the other end down a long incline. "I don't see a house," he commented.

"Of course not," the Oaf boomed. "Nature is my home. I sleep in the grasses against a warm stone or cozy bush, sheltered from the wind." He picked a heart-shaped leaf with small white flowers in the center. "Try some miner's lettuce. It's tasty and good for you."

Faye picked one and devoured it. "It's good," she said, nodding. She picked another one, then another.

Emory finally popped one in his mouth and chewed with a scrunched-up face.

"There are calendulas and dandelions to munch on, plus blackberries, gooseberries, and currants," the Oaf told the children. He motioned for them to follow, leading them on a small path toward the end of the trees. Beyond was a large, golden field where a horse stood alone at the far end next to a fence. A house was perched at the top of a small knoll with ancient oak trees providing shade. He bent down to their eye level. "Now, I want you to meet my dear friends, but you need to be calm and very still. They don't know you yet."

"I'm scared," Faye said.

"A little respect is good, but they won't hurt you if you move slowly, like a turtle." He cupped his ear. "Can you hear them?"

"Maybe," Emory said. "What are we listening for?"

"A buzz."

"Your friends are bees?" Emory asked.

"Yes." He pointed to a majestic oak that reached out in all directions. "In that tree are bees making delicious honey, but more importantly, they pollinate all the flowers that grow the fruit, nuts, and seeds you enjoy eating. Without them, our diet would suffer."

Faye looked up at the tree and wiggled her fingers close to her face.

"Can you feel the tree?" the Oaf asked.

"Not yet."

"You'll get it, keep trying." Sitting with arms around his knees, the Oaf rocked back and forth while gazing out over the field. The air was warm and thick with pollen. After several minutes he stood. "I'm going to talk to my friends now. I want to tell them about a large area of asters in bloom. Also to warn them of the flowers not far from here that have been sprayed with pesticides. If they take nectar from these plants, they will become sick."

He wiggled his body like a dancer warming up before creeping toward the tree. Stopping at the base of the oak tree, he turned facing the direction of the hidden falls and began to waggle his body while moving in a figure eight. Faye and Emory giggled at the sight. Bees swarmed around him in a thick mass. Holding aster flowers in his hands, the bees took turns landing and taking off from the tiny violet petals with a yellow center. The flowers fell from his hands as he changed direction and began dancing in a circle, but now moving backward. Finally, the Oaf dropped to his knees and the bees dispersed. He slowly stood and reached up on tiptoes. Bees buzzed loudly but allowed him to pull off a small golden chunk that hung naked. Bowing, he backed away. Sitting between Faye and Emory while bees flew back and forth over their heads in the direction of the hidden falls, he shared the sweet honeycomb.

CHAPTER 13

SEARCHING

B aba placed her bowl of warm split pea soup on the table and grabbed the newspaper. Flipping it over, a headline caught her eye, *The Oaf Strikes Again*! "Now what's this all about?" she asked herself, with a snort.

> *The elusive Oaf terrorizes the residents of Ophir that live along the creeks, yet again. Leaving trash on their property and caught red-handed stealing …*

"Ahhh, this is such rubbish!" she exclaimed, tossing the paper down. "He'd never do anything of the sort." Lifting the spoon to her mouth, a loud knock rapped on the door. *Who could that be?* she wondered.

Opening the door, a police officer said, "Good afternoon, ma'am."

"How can I help you?" she asked.

"I want to let you know that we will be inspecting your property today. As you know, the Oaf has been seen in your area, and, well, we want to make sure he isn't taking up an abode on your property." He flashed a fake smile.

"Seriously!" she retorted. "You really think this oaf, as you call him, is an actual menace?"

"Not for me to say. Just doing my job, ma'am."

"Very well. Good luck with your search."

"Thanks, ma'am. We won't be long."

Baba closed the door and hustled to her room. She slipped on sandals, put on a hat, grabbed a backpack, and headed to the kitchen. Filling a water bottle, she stuffed it into the pack, along with nuts and a few apples. She grabbed a walking stick and stepped out the back door. With long, deliberate strides, she headed along the trail that led to the road that paralleled the creek.

Finally reaching the bridge, she paused to take a long, deep drink from the water bottle. Wiping her forehead, then grabbing an apple, she crossed the lane and slipped through the foliage where a narrow path followed the creek.

About fifty yards behind, the officer talked on his phone, "I'm following a lead. You keep searching the property and work my way. I'll keep you posted."

Emory walked waist-deep in the pool. Faye leaned against a tree with bare feet wiggling in the water while opening and closing her fingers. The Oaf rested against an adjacent tree with eyes closed and nibbling on a long piece of grass. Emory made his way to the end of the pool and sat on the ledge. He placed his feet in the tumbling water and laughed at the tickle. Faye stared intently at the willow limbs reaching out above his head. She sensed the smooth bark and sturdy stems that secured each long, thin leaf. Her eyes flashed with a devilish grin as she flicked a leaf with her finger.

The Oaf smiled at her success. His ears perked up and he sat forward. Squinting, he peered down the trail at a rustle coming from downstream. Slowly standing, he moved around the tree and peeked out with one eye.

Faye lifted the long limb with her four fingers. Closing her hand, the limb dropped and gently swayed. Her grin became wide as she pressed all her fingertips against her thumb, then quickly opened her hand. The limb rose. She snapped her fingers back against her thumb and the limb swung down, tapping Emory on the head. He swatted at the air. She opened and closed her fingers again. The limb smacked his head. He swatted at the air while looking for the insect that was attacking him. Turning his head down, but keeping his eyes looking up, he saw the limb bending upward.

Just as it dropped, he grabbed the limb, turned and yelled, "Faye! Stop that!"

She giggled with delight.

Baba heard Emory's shout and picked up her pace.

The Oaf remained focused on the trail.

Out of the corner of Emory's eye, he saw someone moving along the trail. "Baba!"

"Emory!" Baba called back.

Faye jumped up, and the Oaf stepped out into the open. They all met by the muddy bank and hugged. "Why have you come?" the Oaf asked with concern.

"The officials are looking for you," Baba answered. "Apparently you upset the wrong person the other day. Something about trash and stealing."

The Oaf waved his hand. "That's grossly bent out of proportion." He smiled at the kids. "That was fun."

"Yeah," they both acknowledged.

"In any event, they're searching the creek for you," Baba said.

"Very well." The Oaf sighed, lowering his head. "I guess it's time to move on for a while."

"Where will you go?" Emory asked.

"Back to the hidden falls."

"Will we see you again?" Faye asked.

The Oaf bent down. "Of course, my fairy. Baba knows where to find me." He promptly stood erect. "Someone's coming."

"I must've been followed," Baba suggested. "That's not good." She hugged the Oaf, then kissed his cheek. "Go. We can manage. You stay safe, hear me?"

He picked up Emory and embraced him. "See you, little man." Bending down, he gazed into Faye's moist eyes. He kissed the back of her hand. "You did well today. Soon, you'll be a real fairy." She grabbed him by the hair and buried her face in it.

"They're getting close, hurry!" Baba warned.

He pried Faye's grasp from his hair and kissed her cheek. "See you all soon." He stepped in the stream and bounded away.

"Well, look who's here!" the officer announced. "Got here quick, didn't you?"

"Yes, officer. I was concerned for my grandkids … after you told me the news of the Oaf."

"You always let small children play alone by the water?"

"No …" she said, feeling silly.

"So where is he?" he asked.

"He?"

"Don't be coy, ma'am." He looked around for footprints. "He was here taking care of them …" he looked at her. "Right?"

"We ran away," Emory interrupted. "Baba wouldn't let us play by the stream alone today, so we snuck out this morning."

The officer glared at Emory.

"Baba always takes us here, so of course she knew where to find us," he continued.

He looked hard at Faye. "Is this true?"

Faye nodded with eyes looking at his feet.

Baba gathered them into her arms. "Would you be so kind as to give us a ride home?"

"What kind of gentleman would I be if I didn't offer you a ride?" He forced a fake smile. "Follow me."

Chapter 14

Magic

"**G**ood morning, sleepyheads," Baba said, peeking through the door. "Your parents will be arriving soon, so have everything packed and ready to go."

"We never got to say good-bye to Bapa," Emory said, rubbing his eyes.

"You have time, if you get up and get out of the house."

"He's here?" he asked, jumping up.

"Waiting for you by our waterfall." Baba leaned against the wall as Emory darted through the door, just missing her, and zipped through the living room and bounded out the door.

"I'll bring you breakfast!" she called. Shaking her head with a smile, she went back into the room. Placing her hand on Faye, who was curled up and breathing heavy under a sheet, she gently shook her shoulder. "Time to get up, sleepyhead."

Faye sat up with a yawn. "Summertime is meant for sleeping in."

"This is true," Baba agreed. "I'd like to take you to the stream before your parents arrive. Would you like to have breakfast by the waterfall?"

"Will the Oaf be there?"

"You never know," she answered, with a wink. "You get dressed and I'll put something together."

Emory stopped at the stream and glanced at all the trees—no knots. His heart sank. Picking up a small, smooth rock, he flung it across the surface and it bounced and landed on the far bank. "Yes!" he said, pumping his fist.

"Well done," the Oaf said, behind him.

Emory jumped with fright. He turned and rushed into his open arms. "You scared me, Bapa!"

"Sorry about that," he whispered. "I understand you'll be leaving today."

"Yes, but I'll be back next summer."

The Oaf sat down, and Emory snuggled next to him. "You're growing up so fast. We all grow up too quickly … and not always correctly."

"What do you mean?" Emory asked.

"We never learn how to remain as a child, inside." He tapped Emory's chest. "It's good to become a man and not act like a child, but we lose our inner child in the process."

"How do I keep from losing it?"

"Well, when we no longer look upon the world with wonder and see its magic, our imagination dims, and we no longer see all the possibilities available. For example, would you like to pet a deer?"

"Of course, but how would we ever get close enough?"

"That's my point. You're not seeing the magic."

Emory lowered his head.

"That's not your fault, it's ours. We need to support your inner child, so you can continue to see, feel, and connect with the magical. Imagination fuels all the possibilities yet to be dreamed." The Oaf walked close to the stream and knelt down. "Sit on my lap," he said, patting his leg.

Emory nuzzled into his warm hug.

"What if we become invisible? Would a deer see us?" he asked Emory.

"No," Emory answered, laughing.

"So, let's become invisible to the deer, and then we can pet it."

"Okay, how do we do that?" he asked, with wide eyes.

"Believe you are invisible by holding very still. Sense the air moving through your body; it feels wonderful."

Emory closed his eyes.

"Do you feel it?"

"You're blocking the breeze," Emory answered. He slid off the Oaf's lap and stood very still. "Yes, I can feel the air flowing through me."

"Good, because a mama deer and her two babies are almost here."

Emory remained motionless with joy spreading through his limbs. A large doe appeared at the top of the hill. Two fawns stepped up behind her. A grin grew on Emory's face and warmed his cheeks. The deer cautiously stepped toward the stream until they stood next to Emory. As the doe bent to take a drink, he placed his hand on her back. She paused with a flicker of her ears and tail, then resumed drinking. He stroked her back, feeling the fur and noting it was coarser than he had imagined. He wanted to pet the babies, but they stood on the other side of her, drinking. The mama lifted her head and sniffed—her ears twitched back. She stepped back and trotted down the trail away from the falls. The two babies followed. Faye and Baba suddenly appeared on the top of the hill. Emory turned to Bapa, but he was gone. Delight bubbled in his chest as the sensation of the breeze now bounced off his skin.

"Thank you, Bapa," he whispered, wondering if the Oaf was still next to him, but invisible.

Faye rushed to the two stick houses still standing at the base of the oak tree. Baba carried her chair and canvas bag to the open ground next to the stream. She opened the chair, then the large bag. "Anyone hungry?" she asked.

Faye rushed to her side.

Emory slowly walked toward her, not wanting to lose the percolating feeling in his body.

They sat and ate in the morning sunshine peeking through the dancing leaves. Baba closed her eyes and listened to the rushing water, reminding her of the continuous breaking of waves at the ocean. Emory sat on the rocks above the waterfall deep in thought. Faye picked flowers and placed them in the stick house made by the Oaf.

A whisper passed by Baba's ears. "I love you."

She looked up at the familiar knot in the oak tree, and whispered back, "I love you, too, my dear."

The knot slid around the tree. Faye giggled, remembering the game. She stood, holding out a purple flower. "This is for you."

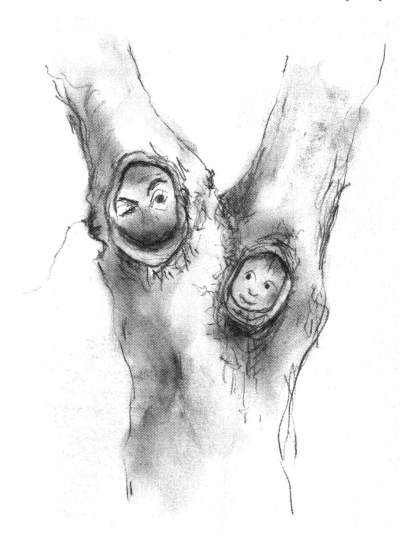

"Thank you. Would you like to join me?" the tree answered.

Faye crinkled up her nose and frowned.

"Want to become a tree?"

She nodded with a large grin.

"Place your back against the tree."

She straddled the stick houses, glanced at Baba, whose eyes were closed, then pressed her back against the trunk. The bark was hard and poked into her skin.

"Feel yourself become the tree and melt into it."

Baba opened her eyes to snickering. She glanced at the stick house and sat up wondering where Faye was. Looking up, she saw two knots in the tree. "Oh my! Nature has another fairy."

About the Author

D aniel received two BAs from University of
California–Santa Barbara; most of his career has
been spent as an IT programmer. In his inspiring stories,
the realm of the magical and spiritual blend with the
heartbeat of all life, and creatures see answers to those
deep questions that stir within us.

Printed in the United States
By Bookmasters